Little
Leaf
Louise

David R Morgan

illustrated by Caterina Cozza

Handwritten inscription: ma – July 2022 & you for all Your help and Support over the years :— & It has been Wonderful working with you – Very best Wishes– David x

Signature: David R Morgan

A2Z PRESS

Little Leaf Louise

Printed in the United States of America

A 2 Z Press LLC

PO Box 582

Deleon Springs, FL 32130

bestlittleonlinebookstore.com

sizemore3630@aol.com

440-241-3126

ISBN: 978-1-954191-57-0

Dedication

*To Bex and Toby
whose love
never
'leafs' me alone!
and to Sue,
for her enduring
friendship*

This Book Belongs To :

_____

When Louise woke up, she was a little leaf.
It was a very windy day.

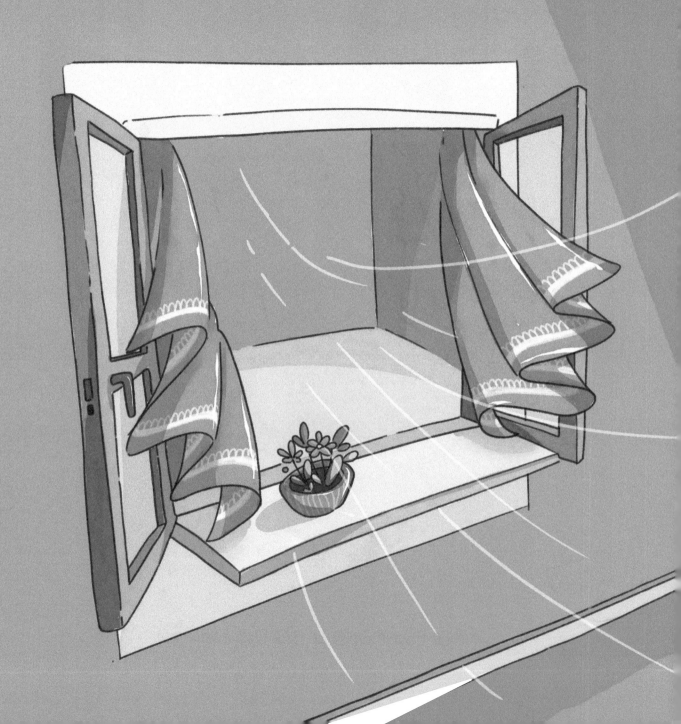

She blew out of her bedroom window
and way down the road, whisking away.

Mum and Dad would have been amazed,
brother Tommy too; but they didn't see and just as well...

as little leaf Louise swirled over cars around lampposts
and between cheeky cats trying to catch her as she rose and fell.

"I think I may go clear across the world!"
She spiralled up to the sky.

Then nearly down to the ground again
and, once more up, up so high.

"Having fun?" asked an oak leaf.
"Yes, thank you," replied Louise.

"I'm Sam," the oak leaf said.
"Follow me, if you please."

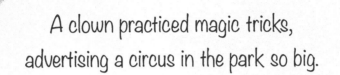

A clown practiced magic tricks,
advertising a circus in the park so big.

As a man on stilts played a trumpet
and a colourful lady juggled an extremely giggly pig.

Before she knew it,
Louise was shooting

down a slide -
"Wheeeeeeeeeee!"

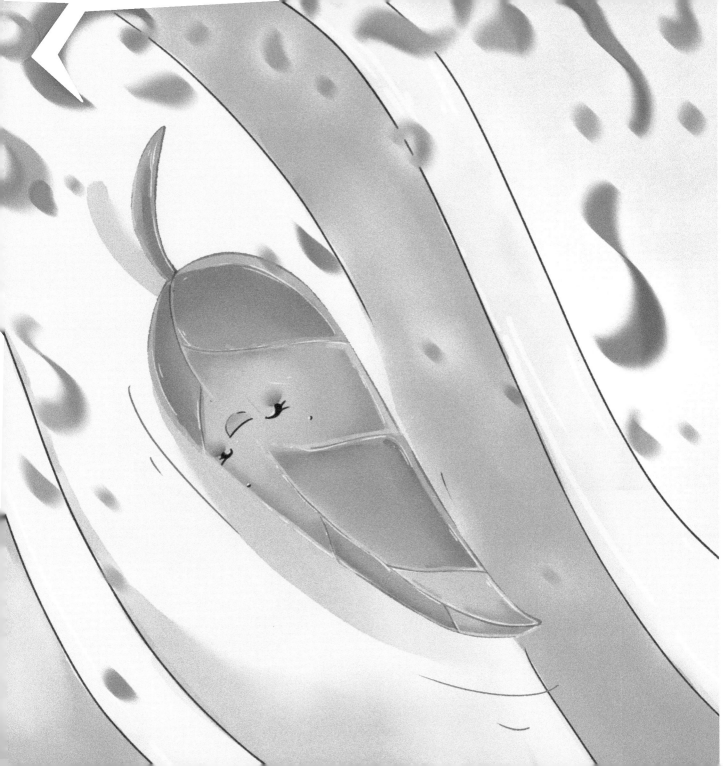

Whirling on the roundabout with Sam,

all around other leaves joined them, she could see.

Then the wind changed, shifting them
out of the park, so down the high street they blew.

Birds raced them and dogs barked
as over the railway tracks the leaves flew.

A train whistled,
speeding away beneath them

as they whisked across a stream and
through a field of wildflowers.

Towards a shimmering wood, where trees
waved happily : *Welcome. Welcome* from their bowers.

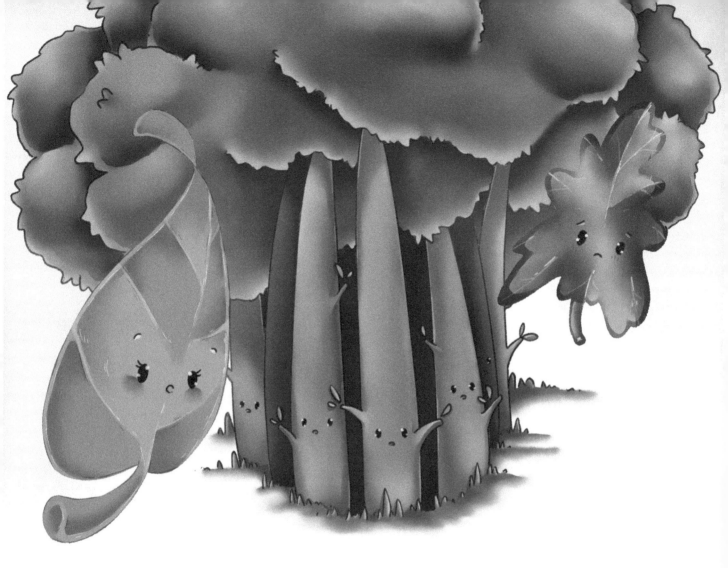

The leaves hovered softly on the breeze.
"The Old One is losing life," all the trees said.

"She has been calling all her children home again,
yet they do not come...just emptiness instead."

"If you young ones could just settle
on her branches for a while, the chance is,

It might just give her life once more."
So one by one the leaves landed on her knotted branches.

"I can feel something,"
Louise said and the rest fluttered.

Life flowed back slowly at first,
then flushed through.

"Thank you," softly spoke the ancient tree. "I can now remember
how it was when I was young and the joy I knew."

The trees all swayed and leaves flurried in cheerful celebration...
But when Louise woke up she was once again a little girl. "Hum,"

"Has it all been just a dream?"
Disappointment gushed through her.

After breakfast she went for a walk with her mum.

Once in the wood, there was the old tree.

It had a single swaying leaf on each branch, yes

The sign of returning life.
Louise smiled.

Mum was engrossed in
sketching wildflowers for a dress.

"Hallo," said a boy. "I'm Sam.
Did you have the same dream too. I was there."

"Yes, I'm Louise and I think we've met before."
And, as they smiled, a magic wind blew through their hair.

The End

The Leaf

A leaf - plural leaves - are collectively referred to as 'foliage,' as in 'autumn foliage.' Most leaves are flattened and have distinct upper and lower surfaces that differ in color, hairiness, the number of stomata (pores that intake and output gases), the amount and structure of surface wax, and other features. Leaves are mostly green in color due to the presence of a compound called chlorophyll that is essential for photosynthesis (how the leaf makes energy - photo for light and synthesis for to make) as it absorbs light energy from the sun. A leaf with lighter-colored or white patches or edges is called a variegated leaf. More fun facts about the leaf or leaves are:

1. A leaf is an appendage (an attached part) on the stem of a plant
2. Leaves are the primary site of photosynthesis - how the leaf makes energy from sunlight hitting the leaf - photo for light and synthesis for to make - this happens in the plant cells in the organ called the chloroplast - which has chlorophyll
3. The photosynthesis process inside a leaf changes water and carbon dioxide into sugar and oxygen when exposed to sunshine, oxygen is used for our needs
4. Leaves can have a many different shapes and sizes that vary between plants
5. The leaves of water plants are specialized to live in the water
6. The leaves of the water-living common duckweed plant (Lemna minor) have some of the smallest leaves in the plant kingdom. Their leaves only reach a length between 0.04 and 0.4 inches.
7. The leaves of the raffia palm plant (Raphia regalis) has some of the longest leaves in the plant kingdom. Their leaves can reach a length of up to 82 feet.
8. A leaf gets its green color from chlorophyll, a green pigment found in chloroplasts
9. In the spring months, plants and trees start to bud and grow new leaves in preparation for the summer months.
10. In the summer months, plants and trees will have leaves that are green.
11. In the fall months, plants and trees start to absorb nutrients from their leaves in preparation for the winter months. Leaves will start to turn into many different colors, including but not limited to yellow, red and brown.
12. In the winter months, plants and trees will be bare and have no leaves. There are exceptions, plants classified as evergreens contain leaves all year round.

There are so many flowers with leaves.
Can you find these flowers and see their leaves?

Orchid

Pansy

Dandelion

Marigold

Carnation

Rose

Stargazer Lily

Violet

Daisy

Calla Lily

Dafodil

Sunflower

Hydrangea

Tulip

Gardenia

Violet

Dahlia

Peony

Lavender

Snapdragon

poppy

chamomile

narcissus

tulip

water lily

jasmine

magnolia

There are so many plants with leaves.
Can you find these plants and see their leaves?

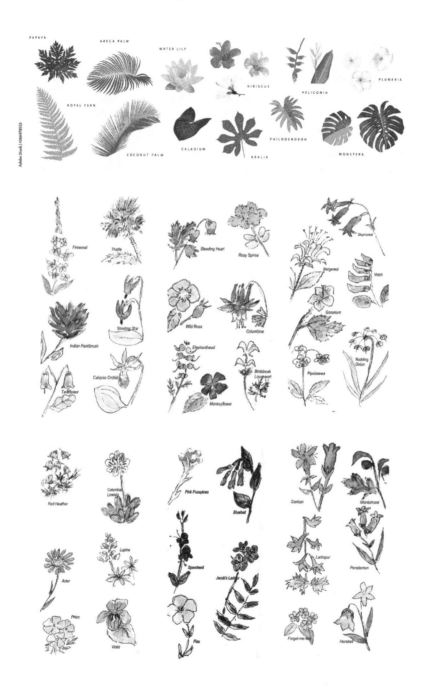

There are so many trees with leaves.
Can you find these trees and see their leaves?

monstera leaf

palmetto fan

sago palm

banana leaf

areca palm

maseangeana leaf

philodendron elephant ear

shell ginger leaf

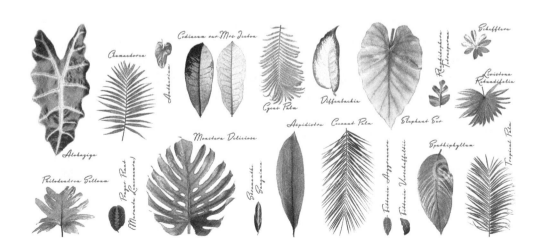

David R Morgan lives in England. He is a talented full-time teacher and writer.

He has written music journalism, poetry and children's books. His books for children include : 'The Strange Case of William Whipper-Snapper', three 'Info Rider' books for Collins and 'Blooming Cats' which won the Acorn Award and was animated for television. He has also written a Horrible Histories biography : 'Spilling The Beans On Boudicca' and stories for Children's anthologies.

For the last 5 years he has been working on his Soundings Project with his son Toby, performing his own poetry/writing to Toby's original music. This work is on YouTube, Spotify and Soundcloud.

Other Books by David R. Morgan

And many more to come!